W9-AMR-170

TO GRAYSON!

EVEN MONSTERS NEED HAIRCUTS

Matthew McElligott

BLOOMSBURY

NEW YORK LONDON OXFORD NEW DELHI SYDNEY

To Christy and Anthony, and to Frank Hodge,
who for twenty-seven years faithfully opened his store every
full moon so the monsters could come in and pick out a book

Copyright © 2010 by Matthew McElligott
All rights reserved. No part of this book may be reproduced or transmitted in any form
or by any means, electronic or mechanical, including photocopying, recording, or by any
information storage and retrieval system, without permission in writing from the publisher.

First published in the United States of America in August 2010
by Walker Books for Young Readers, an imprint of Bloomsbury Publishing, Inc.
Paperback edition published in July 2012
www.bloomsbury.com

Bloomsbury is a registered trademark of Bloomsbury Publishing Plc

For information about permission to reproduce selections from this book, write to
Permissions, Bloomsbury Children's Books, 1385 Broadway, New York, New York 10018
Bloomsbury books may be purchased for business or promotional use. For information on bulk purchases
please contact Macmillan Corporate and Premium Sales Department at specialmarkets@macmillan.com

The Library of Congress has cataloged the hardcover edition as follows:
McElligott, Matthew.
Even monsters need haircuts / by Matthew McElligott. — 1st U.S. ed.
p.   cm.
Summary: At night under a full moon, a child operates a barber shop with a monstrous clientele.
ISBN 978-0-8027-8819-1 (hardcover) • ISBN 978-0-8027-8822-1 (reinforced)
[1. Monsters—Fiction. 2. Barbers—Fiction.] I. Title.
PZ7.M478448Ev 2010   [E]—dc22   2009029916

ISBN 978-0-8027-2801-2 (paperback)
ISBN 978-0-8027-3625-3 (e-book) • ISBN 978-0-8027-3626-0 (e-PDF)

Illustrations created with ink, pencil, and digital techniques
Typeset in Aunt Mildred
Book design by Nicole Gastonguay
Printed in China by Hung Hing Printing (China) Co., Ltd., Shenzhen, Guangdong
6 8 10 9 7 (hardcover)
8 10 9 7 (paperback)

All papers used by Bloomsbury Publishing, Inc., are natural, recyclable products
made from wood grown in well-managed forests. The manufacturing processes
conform to the environmental regulations of the country of origin.

My dad is a barber.
I like to watch him work.
I'm a barber too.

Tonight will be a full moon. I'll need to get to bed early.

Just before midnight, I hear a soft
tapping sound.
Vlad is waiting for me at the window.

I grab my pack and climb down the tree. Together, we cross the fields into town.

I am not allowed out of the house alone.

But I am not alone. Vlad is with me.

Soon we arrive at the alley behind
the shop. I have a skeleton key.

I unpack my supplies. The rotting tonic, horn polish, and stink wax go on the counter. The shamp-*ewww* goes next to the sink.

I tuck the moon powder into my pocket, right next to my tangling brush. I'm ready to begin.

Around twelve thirty, Igor wanders in.

By one o'clock, the shop is full.
It's going to be a busy night.

Some customers are easy.

Some are more difficult.

Some always get the same thing.

Some always want to try something new.

And with some customers, it's tough to know exactly what they want.

Things are going well. Everyone is
getting along. And then it happens.
There is a knock at the front door.
No one ever knocks on the front door.
They all know to come in the back.
Who could it be?

It is a customer. A *human* customer.
We have never had a human customer before.
What are we going to do?

Nobody moves as the man walks to the barber chair.

I am nervous. More nervous than I have
ever been. And then he asks me . . .

"Can you take a little off the top?"

We all have a good laugh over that one.

The sun will be up soon, and the monsters have to go. We sweep up the shop.

We flip back the pictures and turn out
the lights. It's important that we don't
leave *anything* behind.

Some of the guys give me a ride
home.

"See you next month!" I shout.

Soon my dad will be waking up
to go to work. He has his own
customers to take care of.

After all, even humans need haircuts.

Matthew McElligott is the author of many
books for children, including *The Lion's Share*,
Absolutely Not, and two Backbeard the Pirate
adventures. He is not a monster, although he
often dresses like one. His monstrously
talented stylist keeps him looking his best when
he meets his readers. www.mattmcelligott.com

And coming soon to a galaxy near you . . .

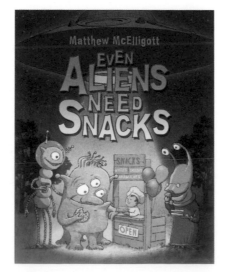